THE TIME TEAM

-THE BEGINNING-

Traveling Near and Far to Find the Truth

―――――――

Sami Kay Starnes

Roman Palace Publishing

Glossary by chapter starts on page 103

For vocabulary lists go to:
http://thetimeteambooks.com/t/vocabulary-lists

To view YouTube channel content please visit:
https://www.youtube.com/playlist?list=PLXjRk4oJQdvr01o
HJCSWFoToXAHC28AKY
See Page 102 In Print Edition

Editors: D. Logan, Morah Sheli Publishing, J. Humphrey
Managing Editor: Devin Starnes
Cover Design: Sam Starnes

13 12 11 10 9 8 7 6 5
ISBN 978-0-692-55680-1

Printed in the U.S.A
This edition first printing, October 2015
TheTimeTeamBooks.com

Dedication

To my husband, my two sons and the one little girl who stole my heart. My mother, my mother-in-law, sisters, father-in-law, brother-in-laws, nieces, nephew, my aunt, and friends who read, read, and re-read until it was perfect – enough for me!
-SKS

Psalms 25:5 – Lead me in your truth and teach me, for you are the God of my salvation; for you I wait all the day long.

Table of Contents

Introduction

My name is Dylan B. Starkes. I live in Los Angeles, California and I am in the fourth grade. I was skipped to the fourth grade because my mom thought *I was not being challenged.* Every morning, she wakes me up and makes me read her a story. Then, she makes me do my math facts. Then, she makes me come and have a conversation with her while she drinks her coffee. It can get rather exhausting.

But hey, now I have friends that are older than me and I love it. I still miss my friends that I had in second grade, but they understand that this is my new class now. When I see them on the playgound, we play like old pals.

For instance, yesterday, I went to play on the yard as normal. I stayed in line all the way until we reached the yard. The wind was blowing so hard that I kept licking my lips. Carla, the meanest girl in the lower grade said, "Dylan, why are your lips so dry and white all around your mouth?" I didn't know what to say. I never understand why she picks on me. So I said, "Because I had a powder donut that I got from *MYYYYYY MOM!*" Everyone laughed so hard.

But they were laughing *at* me. I must admit that was a lame comeback.

I got that joke from my cousin Bo! Bo and I don't get to play that much together because we go to different schools. We have a blast on the weekends. We play everything from cops and robbers to Minecraft and watching "Yo Mama" videos on YouTube. My Aunt Georgia (yes that is her name) always makes us hot dogs. I don't know why she makes us hot dogs all the time. You know, I am allergic to hot dogs. They give me the biggest headache ever by the time I get home.

This year has been hard for me. My teacher keeps telling me that I am too wiggly. I think it's because I am so tired from staying up at night. I honestly do not understand why I have to sit still when no one else is. But I don't say anything. I just try really hard to sit still and *obey* just like my Grandma tells me. SO hard, in fact, that sometimes I sit on my hands. I can't do that for very long because my thumb gets dry and then I HAVE to suck it.

I've sucked my thumb since I was 3 years old. My Aunt Charlate (yes that is her name) sucked her thumb so I thought it would be cool if I did it too. My parents still regret that bad habit I picked up while sleeping over at her house. I tell them all the time that I love sucking my thumb and I too would never stop – well, in my head. I would never tell my parents what I *wasn't* going to do!

Tomorrow we have a field trip to a farm. I get so tired of going to humdrum places like this. I want to go to a museum or a big company and sit in the owner's chair. My Dad said if I don't get in trouble at this field trip and if I am what he considers *"good"*, he will take me someplace fun this weekend. Just him and me! Not me and my mom and him. Not me and my baby sister and him. Just him and me!

Chapter 1

The Stench

I hate riding buses. I don't like being close to people.

We were approaching the farm and Ms. Anderson said, "Alright everyone, put your lunch in the box as you exit the bus."

Immediately Marco stood up and started walking.

"Sit DOWN Marco – have you lost your mind? The bus is still moving!" said Ms. Anderson.

We all started laughing because when the bus stopped, Marco almost fell as he was trying to listen to what Ms. Anderson was saying. He looked so scared. His head was going back and forth like a Dodgers' bobble head. His head was wobbling so much, it looked like it was going to come off.

As he gripped the seats trying to hold on he said, "Ooops, sorry Ms. Anderson, I thought you said get up and go stand in the box."

How could he think *that* I thought?

Then Monica stood up for him and said, "Oh, sorry Ms. Anderson" (in her ever so annoying high-pitched voice), "Marco was so busy looking at *my new* iPad Mini."

She paused to look around at everyone to make sure we all heard her, "That he must not have heard you."

We all gasped. Why? Because first, she is not supposed to have any electronics, and second, where did she get an iPad Mini from? Then again, we all knew exactly where and who she got it from.

Monica's dad owns all of the supermarkets in the town. He even owns the new "organic only" store that sells the smoothies where you can get whatever fruit or vegetable you want. My favorite is the mango, strawberry, and kale.

Once we got off the bus, the smell hit me in the face the same way my baby sister Dallas does when she's happy. It smelled like cow poop wrapped in a fish sandwich with sauerkraut on top. I immediately wanted to rip off my clothes so I wouldn't smell like this when my mother came to pick me up – she is very sensitive to smells. But it was too late.

The stench had already seeped into my clothes and apparently Monica's hair.

"Oooo emmm geee!!! Ms. Anderson, I can't do this! My hair is going to smell like manure."

Monica loves her hair. Everyday she wears it in two afro-puffs and her ribbons always match whatever she is wearing for the day.

"Monica Jenkins, I think your hair will be fine," contested Ms. Anderson.

Monica put her hands over her mouth and said, "But what about my stomach? I can taste how nasty this smells!"

Aminah looked at her and said, "Surely one cannot '*taste*' the way something smells," and rolled her eyes.

"Oh yeah? Then why does your breath smell like you had rotten milk for breakfast?" Monica asked with her arms crossed and a smirk on her face.

"Monica, Aminah…. neutral corners you two!" Ms. Anderson said pointing in two different directions.

I don't know why Monica and Aminah go at it all the time. They argue about the silliest things and try to outdo each other on *everything*.

If Monica gets an "A" on a spelling test, Aminah tries to get an "A+". And they are always in the library after school studying the same subjects. But the funny thing is that they never sit with one another. I think deep down, they really like each other and want to be friends but they just don't know how.

Chapter 2

Bathroom Escort

It is 92 degrees and we are out at the farm? I don't say much in class or ever. I am what most people would call an "introvert." But I must say, THIS IS CRAZY! I feel like I'm going to melt. And these white field trip shirts that our school makes us wear are just ridiculous.

We used to have orange shirts but Monica's mom "suggested", (right before any big change at the school happens, Monica's mom always "suggests" something) that we change to white because it would keep us cool. Which is somewhat true. I mean it's basic physics.

Then again, ultraviolet light passes through (or is blocked by) clothing at the same rate, no matter what color it is....humph. I'm just glad she didn't "suggest" black because black clothing absorbs a lot of heat. So we would be baking right now. Well what do you know, she may have finally gotten one of her suggestions right since white reflects heat.

But who cares about all that!?! I liked the original orange ones. Orange went well with my mohawk and it made me look regal.

Just as I was getting ready to complain about the heat, little miss *prissy* Monica whined, with one hand on her hip and the other fanning her face with her head tilted towards the sky, "Ms. Anderson, it is so hot, I am starting to hallucinate. Can we go back on the bus so that I can play...I mean, so that WE can cool off?"

"No '*you*', I mean '*you all*' may not," she said narrowing her eyes at Monica.

"Remember class, you must either take notes or have a great memory. You'll be using the computer lab to write a report on what you learned about agriculture since the beginning of the quarter. Or, if you like, you can make an animated series," Ms. Anderson explained with her index finger in the air the entire time.

My heart started pounding and thoughts started racing through my head. I wanted to ask if we could do both but I just knew that the class would start clamoring at me. You know...I never really know what they say because every syllable that comes out of their mouths sounds super loud in my head. When they all stare at me, it makes me feel even worse. This is the main reason I don't talk much in school.

And then, *it* happened; the most beautiful girl in the entire universe spoke. Savannah Marie Covington. Her eyes are as brown as my mother's cup of morning coffee. And her hair, well, her hair is always in a high ponytail with an afro-puff at the top. The back is always braided into four braids with beads at the end.

Sometimes her beads are wooden. Other times they are clear. I love the clinking sound of the clear ones and I feel as if I'm in Malawi when she wears the wooden ones. It's like everything she does is in slow motion *and* perfect.

Looking at her, no one would know that she loves everything about sports AND ballet except when she wears my favorite outfit of hers; a Los Angeles Lakers jersey with gold leggings and a purple tutu laced with sequin sparkle at the edges. When she wears *that* outfit, that's when I know her and her father are heading to a Lakers home game right after her ballet class.

I will never forget how radiant she looked at our Christmas program last year. She had her hair braided into two braids with shimmering silver bows at the end. She looked like Princess Ankhesenpaaten (*if* Princess Ankhesenpaaten were to take off her headdress). Her eyes were sparkling when she sang the lead to the Happy Kwanzaa song.

Well, I didn't actually see her while she was singing because I was in the choir. But my father recorded it and I watched it over and over again in awe of her beauty. He missed four calls and three text messages I had it for so long. I didn't even think about downloading a new game I was so mesmerized.

Savannah opened her gorgeous mouth and said, "Ms. Anderson, can we do both a written report *and* an animation?"

Everyone was silent; they never questioned Savannah or her rationale.

"Humm...I never thought about that. Well, if you work with a partner I don't see why not," she agreed.

My heart was so happy! I started making my way through the line to get to Savannah to ask her to be my partner, then I felt something hit my leg. It was my best friend Xavier. He tripped me!

"What the?" I yelled.

Ms. Anderson stopped the line and said, "Dylan, what did you just say?"

I was so scared, I said, "I just wondered why Xavier tripped me so, so, so, so I asked him really loud." What a dope I sounded like.

Everyone was staring at me. Xavier was all the way at the front of the line. There was no way that he could have tripped me. I was so embarrassed I couldn't take my eyes off of Ms. Anderson for fear of everyone glaring at me the way they always do when I speak.

"Dylan, perhaps the heat has gotten to you. Xavier has done no such thing," she said with a confused look on her face.

I know what I felt. *Something* hit my leg. I looked back and I could not believe my eyes. My armpits started to sweat and my heart starting beating over 200 beats per minute. It wasn't Xavier at all. Nor was it mean Carla or any*one* for that matter.

"Ummm, Ms. Anderson, there is a, a, a, SNNNAAAKE!!" I screamed.

Everyone started screaming with me. Ms. Anderson dropped her water bottle and the slimy snake slithered over to it and wrapped itself around the body of the bottle.

Aminah and Monica started holding each other, Xavier starting doing the moonwalk away from the line, and Marco started running in circles.

"Quick everyone run *bus* to the *back*!" Marco muttered.

I was so worried. Not about me, not about Ms. Anderson, and not about anyone else in the class. I was only worried about Savannah. I thought my eyes were deceiving me. But they weren't.

Savannah had picked up the snake and said, "Wait guys, it's just a garter snake. It's not going to hurt you."

The snake was long. It had yellow and red strips and slime was getting all over her hands.

"Eww, the snake is peeing all over her. You are so gross Savannah!" Monica shrieked.

"Not as gross as you are for holding on to your new BFF Aminah," she gloated looking at Monica out of the corner of her eyes and a smug look on her face. Aminah and Monica quickly let go of each other and started brushing off their clothes. Both girls seemed thoroughly disgusted at the fact that they were actually touching each other.

I had to do something to protect Savannah and her good name.

So I spoke up as loud as I could and bellowed, "Snakes don't pee!"

"Everything pees Dylan! Even you in the bed at night," Carla said while laughing and hitting Xavier on the shoulder.

"Ouch girl...or whatever you are," he whispered moonwalking again! But this time *away* from Carla.

Moving closer to Savannah I explained, "No I don't Carla. And neither do snakes."

"Then what's that stuff coming out of its butt?" Xavier inquired.

"Nothing is coming out of its butt. But the slime might be the snake's saliva or venom. It's harmful to snails and stuff but not humans," I articulated with confidence.

I could not believe that the entire class was listening to me. And for the first time they were *looking* at me. They weren't glaring nor carping things I couldn't make out. It actually felt good. Savannah turned her head and smiled at me.

"Dylan is right. I believe only mammals have *all* liquid pee. Reptiles mix their pee and poo. I forget what the name of what it's called but I think it's called 'urates'," Savannah and I said in unison.

I couldn't believe we said "urates" at the same time. I just knew we were meant for each other. And all this time I thought Savannah was only into sports and dancing ballet!

Ms. Anderson swiftly started walking over to us and sternly said, "Savannah, please put that little 'ol nasty reptile down and go wash your hands!"

"Okay Ms. Anderson. But can I hold your hand on *our* way to the bathroom?" Savannah said poking out her lip and pretending to chase her.

Ms. Anderson did an about-face, threw both her hands in the air and started squealing like a pig and ran behind the sign that said, *"Welcome to Logan Farm Ms. Anderson's class."*

We all started pointing at Ms. Anderson and howling with laughter.

Hugging herself and breathing hard, Ms. Anderson gesturing Savannah towards the gift shop and commanded, "Heck no little girl! Oooooo-weeee. Get out of here and hurry back!"

Chapter 3

Focus

"Hey Dylan!" Xavier yelled running over to me.

"Was that stuff you said true about snakes? Or were you just sticking up for your girlfriend?" he whispered.

"No, it's true and she's not my girlfriend," I hissed.

"Wow, I didn't know Savannah was *that* smart. I'm going to ask her to be my partner. That way, she can do the written part and I can do the animation baby!!!" Xavier said with both hands up in the air like someone had made a touchdown and gyrating his hips in the wind.

I was stunned. I didn't know what to say. I wanted to say, *"Noooooo – please, please, please let me ask her."*

But I didn't. Instead I said, "Oh, I think that will be a great idea. Don't forget to take notes," with a half smile as I snapped my fingers and pointed toward him as if I was scolding him.

I threw my head back and my shoulder sank. Another opportunity to get to learn more about Savannah missed.

Savannah made it back and we were on our way. Ms. Anderson introduced the farmer to us. And she was a girl! I never knew girls could take care of a farm.

"Who has ever visited a farm?" the farmer-lady asked.

Monica raised her hand and without being called on said, "My family and I go every year to get me *my own personal* pumpkin and to take fall photos."

Why oh why she swings her shoulders when she talks I will never know.

"Very well. Anyone else?" farmer-lady queried.

"Wait, I wasn't finished. *And* we send my daddy's workers to a farm each and everyday to get only the freshest fruits and vegetables for the grocery store *chain* we own..."

The farmer-lady cut Monica off in mid-sentence. Poor Monica, she so looked disappointed that no one else was listening to her speak. You would think she'd be used to it by now.

"Perfect, anyone else," the farmer-lady said moving away from Monica.

"I went to a dairy farm and learned how to milk a cow and feed baby goats once," Xavier interjected.

"Great. Well this farm is called an *organic fruit farm*," the farmer-lady said.

I am sure what she said after that was very interesting, but I started daydreaming – a cooing noise began in my head. I started thinking of ways to get Savannah to ask *me* to be her partner before Xavier got to her. I thought about asking my Aunt Georgia to make me a shirt that says, *I'm great at animation and writing papers, ask me to be your partner.* But that would take too long. I needed to quickly figure out a way to make it happen TODAY...and before Xavier.

Just when I had the greatest plan ever, I heard, "Dylan, what do you think could make one?" Ms. Anderson asked.

"Make what?"

"Were you not listening Dylan?" Ms. Anderson asked.

"I think banana peels and egg shells would make great compost Ms. Anderson," Savannah answered smiling at me.

"Thank you Miss Savannah, but I was asking Dylan. Dylan, why don't you come stand next to me so that you can focus better?" Ms. Anderson said.

I *was* focused, just not on this boring field trip.

Chapter 4

Stuck

Finally, after dissolving like sugar in hot water for what seemed like hours, it was time to go. Ms. Anderson told us to gather all of our things and to start walking towards the bus.

"Move, I need to make sure I get the same seat," Carla said pushing everyone out of her way.

"No pushing or talking 'crazy' to people kids!" said Ms. Anderson.

"I am not a kid!" Xavier announced.

Everyone let out a loud "oooooo" because we just *knew* Ms. Anderson was going to let Xavier have it.

She put both hands on her hips, leaned down, walked towards Xavier and said, "Well, Mr. Xavier, if you are not a kid, then what are you?"

"I'm a child," he said sheepishly.

"Same difference, let's get on the bus. I'm hot," Monica mumbled lightly brushing pass Xavier.

"A 'kid' is a baby goat. I am a child," Xavier now said with a little more confidence.

I smiled at Xavier and was very pleased. He was absolutely right. He didn't back down and he was respectful (something he has a hard time doing at times.)

"Then that must make you a baby human," Marco said looking towards the sky as if he was trying to count the clouds.

"Yup!" I said standing next to Xavier like a bodyguard.

"Fair enough – *children*, get your baby human butts on the bus!" Ms. Anderson ordered with a fake smile on her face.

Just when Xavier was getting ready to say something else, everyone told him to be quiet and to just do what she asked. We all sat down and I heard the bus driver complaining about something to Ms. Anderson.

Our bus driver, Mr. Devin, has always driven us to our field trips. He is the nicest driver I know and the only driver I know at my dad's company. He always has cold water and his bus always smells like pinecones. The only time it doesn't is when we go to see *Debbie Allen's Hot Chocolate Nut Cracker*; then the bus smells like peppermint – I LOVE IT!

The bus was really loud with everyone talking and laughing. That's when we heard a loud CLANK-CLANK-CLANK noise. We all got quiet. Everyone's eyes grew from dime size to half dollar in seconds. Then, our eyes started doing one-eighties. Mostly with our heads out of the window hoping an alien wasn't trying to abduct the bus.

Then we heard it again. *CLANK-CLANK-BOOM!* White and gray smoke started dancing out of the engine first on the left side and then on the right.

Ms. Anderson jolted her head up and had an alarming, never seen before, crease on her forehead that looked like three fingers were fighting and roared, "Umm, what in the world was that?"

"I'm sure it's nothing that I can't fix. Give me about ten minutes to check it out," Mr. Devin said.

"Oh my gosh! I hope we don't get stuck here. I have a play date planned with Breeauna Buchannan today," Monica said fanning herself.

Savannah looked at her and said, "Oh really? I have a play-date with her too today. Is her mother coming to get us both?" she asked looking *very* confused.

"I have no idea, my nanny set it up with her nanny," bragged Monica.

"Oh. Well, don't worry. I am sure everything will be ok," Savannah said with a smile. (I wonder if Savannah not having a nanny had something to do with the play date mix up.) She is always so positive.

In a condescending tone, Ms. Anderson faced Xavier and said, "Children?"

Xavier gave Ms. Anderson a look of approval.

She turned her back to him and continued, "I need to step off the bus and make a phone call to the school to let them know we'll be a little late. I trust that all of you will act like you have good sense and not make me have to come back on this bus and wreck shop."

Just then, Marco's hand goes up.

"Yes, Marco," Ms. Anderson said breathing heavily pointing towards him.

"I never felt the bus move. Did we really wreck it by running into a shop?"

We all started belly laughing.

"She means she wants us to be on our best behavior while she makes her call Mar-COOOOO!!!" exclaimed Aminah with an annoyed look on her face and shaking her head.

Ms. Anderson nodded her head toward Aminah and said, "Right!?!"

Now she too was shaking her head.

Just then, we all heard Ms. Anderson say to Mr. Devin, "Hey Dev, let me borrow your phone. I don't have any service out here for some reason."

Mr. Devin came from under the bus and started handing her his phone.

He stood up, wiped his eyebrow with his shoulder, put his finger in his ear and said, "Well, I don't have very much battery left. This isn't my bus. There was a mix up at the yard and someone took *my* bus with all stuff in it like my charger, my water, *and* my incense for crying out loud."

"Really? I *thought* something was different when we got on and it smelled like leather, rotten shoe polish, and throw-up," Ms. Anderson said smiling and holding her hand out to receive Mr. Devin's phone.

Chapter 5

Rescued

It's getting dark; we are all hungry and tired. I cannot *believe* its been this long - over two hours. I thought one of our parents would have come in search for us by now. Ms. Anderson's cell phone had no service and Mr. Devin's phone was completely dead.

We tried to send an email from Monica's iPad Mini but there was no Wi-Fi – even though she *swears* her father only buys her the *best of the best*. Obviously he doesn't if she didn't have a data plan attached to her device.

I really want to get home. All my real friends are there. My mother always accuses me and the things in my room of anthropomorphism. I always smile at her and make sure I keep my door closed. I think my father knows my secret. He always winks at me when I come out of my room or when I am carrying one of my friends...I mean pets.

Suddenly, my jacket pocket started moving. I quickly slapped it.

"Ouch man," Bello said.

My heart started racing. Bello must think I'm home already. I started coughing very loudly.

"Dylan, are you ok?" Savannah asked.

"Ewww! Cover your mouth NASTY!" Carla yelled.

"Um yes, yes, I'm ok. I just had something in my throat," I replied with my head down.

With a concerned look on her face Savannah asked,

"Do you want me to ask Mr. Devin for some water?"

"No, no. I'm good. I'm just tired and want to go home," I said turning towards her.

Just then, my pocket started moving again. I had to think of something quick. My heart was thumping so hard and my mind was racing so fast I didn't even hear what Savannah was saying to me. I saw her mouth moving but I just couldn't make out the words.

"Well, do you?" Savannah asked with a worried look on her face.

"Do I what?" I said with a crooked smile.

"Do you think we will ever get to go home?" she repeated.

"Oh, of course we will. This situation will be fixed in no time," I said with a reassuring voice.

At that very moment, I was elated to see Xavier. He walked up and was his normal loud self and asked, "What's up p-e-o-ples?"

"Oh nothing much, just sitting here worried that we won't get out of here," she explained.

"I know Dylan isn't worried," he joked slapping me on my back. "He never worries about anything. He gets good graaaaaades, he's smaaaaart and he's handsome, don't you think Savannah?" he said shaking his head up and down with a grin.

I jerked my head up and glared at him. I could not believe he just said that. I mean, what was he trying to do, embarrass me in front of all people; Savannah?

"I'm just kidding. You don't have to answer that Savannah," he said smiling with both hands behind his neck looking at her with low eyes.

"Shame. I think he would've liked my answer," she said with a smile - and slowly turned away from me.

It seemed like the longest smile ever.

Then we hear, "Thanks be to glooory! We are getting out of here!" Ms. Anderson was throwing her hands up to the sky and waving them with her eyes closed.

We all started screaming like we were on a roller coaster.

She laughed one good time and said, "Hey, hey, hey! My hearing aid is already set to ten. I do not, and I repeat, I do not want to know what reverberation FEELS like!" while covering her ears.

Chapter 6

Hello Bello

The bad part about being this late is that we get stuck in what my father calls "rush hour traffic. "

"You know I'm hungry right?" Bello said.

"Shhhhhh..I'm not home yet," I said turning closer to the window in my seat of the bus.

"Why not man?" Bello hollered

"I said shhhhush!"

"It's almost 5 o'clock," Bello whispered.

Talking into my pocket I said, "I know, but something happened to the bus – now quiet down before someone hears you!"

"Then why do I hear SpongeBob in the background?" Bello whispered.

"Just hush your face!" I insisted.

"Aye dude...I don't have a face remember," Bello yelped.

"No, I don't remember that – but you should remember that no one knows about you so please, please, please, be quiet until we get back home!?!" I said talking through my teeth.

"Okay, okay, okay...just tell me why I hear SpongeBob in the background and I'll leave you alone, I promise," Bello begged.

"First, you DO have a face. You just have never seen it because you change it so much and the SpongeBob you hear is Monica's iPad," I answered getting more and more annoyed at each exchange.

"Whhhaaat? She has an iPad?" Bello said sounding surprised.

With my teeth clenched I ordered, "Yes! Now go away!"

"Sorry about the delay parents, we had some minor mechanical problems. Thank you all for waiting," Ms. Anderson said playing with her bangs as she helped us off the steps of the bus.

"Well, a call would've been nice!" Monica's nanny said as she pulled Monica away.

"Hey Xavier," I called out. "Want to come over to my house and play?"

Just then my pocket started to move and I jumped a little.

"Naa – I can't. I have to find a way to ask Savannah if she wants to be my partner. And this is my weekend to be with my dad. I don't want to miss another minute of it," he screamed running off and waving at me.

"Oh, that's right, I forgot. Okay, then I'll see you Monday," I said waving back knowing he couldn't see me.

It was getting dark and I really wanted to get home before it got too cold so I could feed Bello. Just then, I realized that no one was there to pick me up. I looked towards the parking lot and I saw Savannah was waiting as well.

She walked over to me and said, "Hey Dylan. I thought your mom comes to pick you up everyday?"

"Well, I thought your sister comes to get you everyday too."

"She does. I guess she's late today," she said with a worried look on her face.

"Well, you can come to my house and call her. My cell phone is dead," I offered.

"Mine too. Are you allowed to walk home alone?" Savannah asked sniffling and wiping her nose with the back of her hand.

With a smile so big that my teeth got dry I said, "Well, we'll find out when I get there. Come on, I'll carry your bag."

I was smiling *so* hard at times that my top lip got stuck to my gums. I'm sure I looked like an old man when he takes his dentures out and *Fire Marshall Bill* all rolled into one person. I didn't care. I was just happy to be spending time with Savannah outside of school.

Chapter 7

Ewww...

"Dylan, how did you get here?" my mom asked.

"We walked."

"Who is *we*?" She said coming around the corner looking *very* concerned while wiping her hands on her apron.

"Mom, meet Savannah. She's in my class," I said taking her coat.

"Weeeeeell, well, well. So *this* is Miss Savannah," my mother said sucking her teeth and smiling at the same time.

"Okkkkaaaayyyy – Savannah let's go to my room," I said grabbing her hand and heading to my room.

"Whoa, whoa, whoa! Your room? Boy you must be crazy. Savannah, does your mother know that you're here?" My mom asked.

Politely, Savannah responded, "Um, I'm not sure. May I call my father from here?"

"Yes. Use my cell phone on the table over there and don't hang up when you're done. I want to talk to him," my mother said pointing her finger to the phone.

When we walked into my room, I looked at the clock and realized that we only had 45 minutes to play *and* to get *her* to ask *me* to be *her* partner for the report. *She* had to ask *me* so Xavier wouldn't be mad at *me* for asking *her* before *him*.

She walked into my room, looked around as if she had walked into a spaceship and said, "Wow, your room is so empty. Why don't you have any toys?"

"I do, they're just in my closet. I need my room for..."

And before I could finish, Bello jumped out of my pocket. Savannah screamed like she had seen a ghost or as if someone was trying to kidnap her. She started throwing pillows at him, stomping her feet, running in circles and surrendered by covering her ears with her shoulders. She was so loud; my mother came running down the hall. I met her at the door and poked my head out.

"Yes mom," I said.

"What was that noise? Was that Savannah screaming?" she said trying to peek into my room on her tippy-toes.

"Yes, it was. She saw my lizard," I confessed hoping that would stop her from wanting to come inside.

"Oh, okay. Well, I am here if you need anything sweetheart. I hate that little smelly thing too. And keep this door open. The day you pay a bill is the day you can close your door," my mom said pushing to door open and talking to Savannah.

She must have forgotten daddy had not fixed it yet and it eased right back closed.

"Whaaaat, she hates me?" Bello cried.

Trembling, Savannah scaled the wall toward my closet and yelped, "Wait, that *thing* can talk?"

I immediately felt hot. I even felt like I had the bubble-guts. Like I needed to use the bathroom and stay in there for more than 40 minutes. Not only was my stomach turning, my ears were getting hot too.

I had to say something but only "Ummmmmmm" came out of my mouth.

Think about it. For the first time, Savannah and I are alone AND she is in my room AND she is meeting Bello for the fist time AND she's finding out he's more than just a lizard – he can talk. Now, mix that with Bello being devastated to finally find out that my mother hates him.

"I knew it. I had a *strange* feeling that she was always trying to kill me. No, no...starve me. Oh I don't think I can live here anymore. I am *offended*! I am *devastated*! I love yo' mama. Oooo, you know I do. I am the one that gave her the idea to lock her hair and this is how she treats me?"

Bello was pacing back and forth on the windowpane talking to himself.

Savannah looked like she both stepped in and smelled sewer water.

"Okay, sit down," I tell her.

"But not over by Bello. He's irrational right now. And he tends to poop everywhere when he is nervous or, in this case *devastated*. Come over here and put your back against my bed on the floor."

Savannah moved very slowly towards my bed. Bello crawled higher up the window and looked like he was going to cry.

Shaking his head back and forth he continued, "All these years I've been in this house. Tending to her. Listening to her horrible singing. Watching her make hair oils! I thought your mom loved me!" he rambled on and on. "OOoooooOOOoooo. She changes my poop thingy ever so carefully and gently when *you* forget. And here I was thinking she was enjoying spending time with me that's why she was going so slow. NOW I KNOW THE TRUTH! I remember the day like it was yesterday when I peed on her. She just ran her fingers through her dreadlocks and pretended like it never happened," Bello sobbed.

"Ewwww," we both said.

"That is disgusting!" Savannah said holding her mouth.

"That never happened and you know it Bello," I said, glaring at him showing him just how embarrassed I was.

"Okay, you're right. It never happened. But now that I *know* she doesn't like me, the next time she changes my poop I *will* pee on her for sure!" he said with a maniacal laugh.

"Okay – now I am freaking out!" Savannah yelled.

"Shhhh! Please don't. Let me explain," I begged crawling over to her.

"I'm listening," Savannah said folding her arms scooting away from me.

"Bello is my best friend. People think that he is just a rock that I carry around everywhere. But Bello can transform into anything I need. So, when we are at home, he is a lizard. When we are at school, he is just a pebble. Or if I need an eraser, he is an eraser," I said with my hands behind my back waiting for her to run out the door.

Savannah looked at me like she knew something that I didn't.

Closing in on me Savannah crossed her arms and taunted me saying, "Sooo then you're *not* as smart as everyone thinks you are. You're a cheat! And you have your little minion, *Belly*, or whatever his name is, to help you with everything! You are despicable Dylan B. Starkes and I am going to tell everyone!"

This time she was staring at me straight in my eyes.

"No, no. *Bello* is his name, and it's not like that. I am not a cheater. I really *am* as smart as people think I am and a little more if you asked Bello," I explained.

"Are you sure? You said he can transform into anything so why wouldn't he transform into correct answers for a test?" Savannah said pouting her lips.

Chapter 8

Rules

"First, Bello has some rules that he comes with. One –
he cannot help me academically. Two – he cannot help me
with love or to be liked or to have money. Three - he is his
own person. He can come and go as he pleases," I
explained.

"Where did you get him? Like, how did you find out he
could do all of this?" she asked inquisitively.

"I found him on our trip to South Africa to see
Mandela's inauguration."

"Wait, why did you go to Africa to see that? You're not
African!" she said with a confused look on her face.

"Well, *I* may not be from Africa, but my ancestors are
and so are yours," I said in a mater-of-fact tone to her.

I was so happy she asked *why* and not *when* because
Mandela's inauguration was over 20 years ago.

"No they are *not*," she said looking demented.

"Yes, they are. Bello told me so. As a matter of fact his
name means 'assistant' in Swahili. That's all he is here to

do for me...assist," I said (hoping she will understand and believe me.)

"Oooooo! Like Chris Paul on the Clippers?" she said enthusiastically.

"Yeah – just like CP3!"

"I'm listening," she said with her arms still crossed.

"How did you meet him and how did you find out that he could do all this stuff?"

"You're not gonna let it go, huh?"

"Nope!"

"Riiiiiight. So I was walking in a village in South Africa and I spotted this yellow flower that I was going to pick for my mother. I knew something wasn't right because I got a weird feeling in my stomach. The wind started to blow and I thought I heard my father's voice. Just as soon as I plucked it out of the ground and started to smell it, this large tree sprang out of the ground and it lifted me up beyond the clouds. Slowly I heard a voice say, 'Dylan Bishop Starkes, what are you doing here son?' Surprisingly, I wasn't scared. We talked for what seemed like forever. He told me stories and special places to visit if I ever got the time. He revealed secrets of ancient times and believe it or not, I felt at peace throughout the entire visit."

"I don't!"

"Ah-ha. Well, to make a long story short he told me to go back down the tree. And when I was almost down, he threw this pebble at me and said that it would protect me and guide me all of my days. I was not sure if he was talking about himself."

"Who?"

"You know the guy that was talking to me, or the pebble. So I just caught it and ran to tell my mother."

"But why were you in a field looking for flowers? And I thought you needed a *Passbook* to be out alone in the streets of South Africa if you were Black. This doesn't sound right Dylan! Who goes to Africa and looks *for* *f*lowers in a *f*ield? Where were your parents?" Savannah asked apprehensively and put a lot of force on the "*fs*" for some reason.

"Are you talking about a dompas?" I asked.

"You better stop cursing before your mom comes in here!" she warned.

"I'm not cursing. It was called a Passbook and a 'dompas', I'm serious." We both chuckled.

"I am too. But I'm talking about the Passbook. P.A.S.S.B.O.O.K," pretending to read the palms of her hands.

"No, those were done away with around 1986, my mom told me. That's why it was so important to go see the inauguration. Mandela fought for equality. And the weird thing was that when this law was done away with..."

"Which law?"

"The dompas one."

Smiling she interjected, "I said stop cursing."

"Okay. I'll say Pass Law instead. The sad thing was that, Mandela was still in jail when the law was repealed. And that's what *I* wanted to go see when we were there. I wanted to go to a museum, you know, where I could see a real Passbook with my own eyes but noooooooooo...they both were too busy. My dad had business to take care of and my mother was painting."

"What was she painting?"

Dang-it, why is she asking me all these questions????

"I don't know. And at the time, I didn't care. I just wanted out of that stuffy room."

"What did your dad do? You two are always together. Why didn't he take you with him?"

"I told you. He had business to take care of."

"So he just left you there with nothing to do? Did you have a computer at least? An iPad, a Nook, a Kindle, a phone, anything?"

"That's a negative. He saw I was mad but I still couldn't go with him. I hate art. And the thought of having to sit and *watch it come alive* was NOT my idea of vacation fun."

"Well, that's obvious," she said looking around at the bare walls in my room.

"So what did you do? Get to the point! That thing is over there banging on the window like a mad*thing* and starting to freak me out. So your dad just made you sit there?"

"No. He told me I could go outside. But only to one particular side of the field – the side where my mom could see me while she was painting."

"Let me guess...you didn't right?"

"Let's just say I snuck out. And well, *now* I know that on the other side of the flower was an animal trap," I said with my head down.

"So, you got rewarded for doing something you weren't supposed to do?"

"I guess so. But when I was talking to the voice, he scolded me for not listening to my parents and he is the one that showed me the abyss on the other side. The light that led me up explained why I had to be higher than the trap to see it. I guess that is why the tree appeared and scooped me up. Without it, I would have been gone forever. Man, the light that took me up was so bright, I thought I was following a star in the night's sky."

There was dead silence for about 15 seconds. Even Bello had stopped mumbling to himself. It was awkward for sure. But at least she had stopped with the questions!

We had ten minutes left until Savannah's dad was due to pick her up.

Savannah jumped up and said, "Although your story sounds suspicious, we have to make a pact! Like the Mayflower Compact. Or better yet, something that says *I* will not tell anyone if *you won't* tell anyone."

"That sounds great – people already think I'm a weirdo, I don't want this added to their lists of names they have for me," I said holding my head down even lower this time.

"Hey, chin up Dylan B. Starkes. People don't call you names. If anything, they *wish* they were you. I mean think about it. You sir, are going to be finished with school a whole year before you're supposed to. Which meansssss, you're going to spend less time in school, *and* you get to start college early," she said flopping down on my bed.

I never looked at it that way. But I know I hear people saying things about me when I walk by in the cafeteria. I guess I'll have to start listening more closely.

"Well, that's good to know," I said.

Just then my mom came in to tell Savannah her dad was here. Dang it, I thought. I didn't get a chance to ask her to be my partner.

Instantly, I heard Savannah announce, "Daddy, I need to come over here this weekend. Dylan and I have our year-end gardening report to do on the farm and we are doing a written report *and* a short film. Ms. Anderson said we HAVE to have partners."

She winked at me, did some ballet move where she crossed her ankles, put her arms out, and bowed to me the way people do to show respect in Japan, Korea, Taiwan, China, and Vietnam.

SUCCESS!!!!!!

Chapter 9

Reconstruction

My mom listens to this song that says, *"It never rains in Southern California"* every time it rains – in SOUTHERN CALIFORNIA. I could not believe that just days ago it was 92 degrees and now it is raining. And because I didn't get in trouble at the farm, my dad and I were venturing someplace special today. I hope he doesn't change his mind because of the weather. The last thing I want to do on my Saturday, other than my Saturday art class, is to miss the opportunity to be with my dad all by myself.

Just as I was staggering out of my bed to ask him where we were going, I opened the door and my dad jumped out of nowhere and scared the crap out of me.

"What's up Dyllllll?" My dad said as he jumped up and down, up and down.

Confused, I glared at him and said, "You! Over and over again it looks like! Daddy stop jumping, I just woke up and everything is fuzzy to me."

"Why? I am practicing for our outing today. Just you....me....and some orange socks baby-baaabbbbaee," he said with a smile as he continued to jump.

"Yes!!! Skyzone!!!" I said screaming and jumping up and down with him.

"Shhhhhh – I told your mother I was taking you to the art store to get some supplies. I convinced her that it would help *motivate* you for your upcoming class," he said leaning down with his finger over his lips.

Gleaming I said, "Oh, okay, I am going to put my clothes on *right* now."

Just then, my mother walked past and said, "Why ya'll all whispering and stuff?"

While snickering, Daddy replied, "Oh, no reason Sugar-Dumpling. Dylan was just getting ready to wash his face and brush his teeth. I told him to brush them the way he is going to brush the new canvases we're buying today," and he kissed my mom on the cheek.

"Umm, humm," she said pulling away from him looking at him up and down.

"What? Can't a man and his son spend some quality time together talking about art?" He grabbed her coffee cup out of her hand and took a couple of sips from it while looking at her over the rim. Handed it back to her and kissed her on the other cheek.

My mom giggled and said, "Well, I guess not. You are such a good man, Mr. Starkes."

"A good man, who married a great woman, and had some wonderful children!"

She leaned in to kiss him on the lips and I pried my head between them and asked, "Can we bring Sanura? We can tell them she's a service cat."

I pretended to please with my hands clinched together. I could feel my mom's heart beating on the back of my head and my dad's coarse chest hairs on my forehead as I tried to pry them apart.

"Of course not! And there's no a such thing as a 'service cat.' Leave her here to keep Dallas and Mommy company on this raining day while we go shopping for *art supplies,*" he said loudly, gesturing air quotes as he yelled the words *art supplies.*

I was so excited! I didn't care if Sanura came or not, I just wanted to roll out and right now. I didn't want to brush my teeth or do any of my "morning business" as my mom calls it. I just wanted to sprint out and wait in the back seat of the car like a psycho in a horror movie.

Only I would not try to harm my dad. I would just pressure him to drive like my mom trying to get to the library before it closed – fast! This way, we would be the first ones there. You know, *before* it started to smell like sweaty fungus feet and burnt day-old popcorn.

When the doorbell rang I thought it was my Aunt Georgia coming over to talk about who knows what. But the voice I heard made my stomach drop. It was Xavier. Noooo, nooo, nooo! Not today. Today, I wanted my dad all to myself. Then I heard a girl's voice. I couldn't believe it, he had Savannah with him.

"Dylan!!" my mother called out. "Miss Savannah and Xavier are here to see you."

What the heck? I thought. Why are they here? It's a Saturday. Xavier is supposed to be with his dad and dang-it I am busy! I stormed to the door fast and annoyed. My fists were pumping north and my elbows were jerking south about six good times all while I was huffing and puffing. Savannah looked down and started laughing.

Just then, Xavier said, "Ahhh, dude? I know you love Spiderman and all, but we don't need to know exactly how much. So, you might wanna go put on some pants."

Aww fish-chips, I forgot I was in my underwear (or my *draws* as my mom calls them). I ran back to my room and tried to cover my butt with the throw pillows from the couch. But you know what? At this point, I wouldn't care if they saw my bare butt. If that is what it would take for them to *get ghost,* so that my dad and I could leave, then so be it.

I felt like mooning them from here to New York. Luckily, I made it to my room without anyone feasting their eyes on my booty. But I was still upset. I don't like when people just "drop by."

I fell about three times trying to put my pants on and just settled on a pair of shiny, gold basketball shorts.

"Do you want me to go and see what they are talking to your mom about?" Sanura purred as she jumped into my lap.

"No, I just want them to leave!" I said debating whether or not I wanted to go back out into the living room and get them. I couldn't gather myself to move from my floor.

"Did I just hear you say you *wanted* thee Miss Savannah to leave?" Bello inquired.

"Yes! Skyzone is calling my name. They were not invited and I don't feel like being bothered. I had a long night last night. I was learning about the Reconstruction and a whooooollle bunch of stuff that happened after it. I even got the chance to talk to Pap himself to ask why people were calling it the Exodus and him an 'Exoduster.' We laughed at the name because at first I thought they were calling him a duster...you know the kind you clean with, get it – get it?" I chuckled and looked at them back and forth.

Bello nor Sanura were amused.

"Pap spent a great deal of time explaining to me why Kansas was a better place to migrate. And why Black people didn't want to stay in Nashville since the war was over," I continued.

"You act like we weren't there. Your little Exoduster crack, well, it wasn't funny then and it's not funny now. Your jokes are pretty corny friend," Bello said.

About ten minutes passed. Bello and Sanura had to nearly force me to go get them from the living room and find out why they were here.

I walked out of my room and my dad was smiling from ear to ear.

"Dylan, you didn't tell me you were expecting company."

With an angry and confused look on my face I said, "I *wasn't* expecting them!"

"Well, Mr. Starkes, I forgot my bracelet in Dylan's room yesterday and Xavier walked me over to get it," she said politely.

Bracelet, I don't remember seeing no dang bracelet in my room. I don't even remember her having a bracelet on yesterday. And I notice everything about her. What were they up to?

"Oh, Dylan go get it. Hopefully that little nasty lizard didn't get to it by now," my mother said while peeking over her computer screen.

"Ummm, I have to go get it, I don't think Dylan knows where it is," Savannah said.

What the heck was going on? Something fishy for sure and I was not happy about it one bit. I *hate* not knowing what's going on. Suddenly, Savannah grabbed my hand and literally dragged me to my room while Xavier moonwalked past my parents with both his hands in his pockets smiling and nodding.

Chapter 10

Handy Dandy Thumb

Xavier shut the door and said, "Alright, where is he?" looking behind my bed.

"Where is what?" I said looking at both of them like they were as crazy as fig beetles that kept running into walls.

"The talking lizard! Savannah said you have a lizard that can talk. Bro, we've been friends since Tiny Tots! Man, I used to cover for you when you peed on your cot. Dude, you haven't even told *me* you have a talking lizard, but you tell *her*? What's up with that? Are you mad at me or something?" Xavier said opening up my drawers and peeking out the window.

I glared at Savannah.

She put one shoulder up to her ear, and reached both arms out in an attempt to touch me and said, "Now Dylan, in all fairness, we never made our pact. And it just came out."

"Oh really? How does something like this just *come out*?" I asked.

"Xavier called me last night to ask me if I would be his partner and I couldn't hold it in," she confessed.

I started breathing so hard; it felt like I needed to get my asthma inhaler from the car. If I had it right now, I would take FOUR big puffs.

"It's okay Dylan, really it is. I swore Xavier to secrecy and I thought he already knew. Like he said, you two *have* been friends since Tiny Tots," Savannah continued.

"Well, so have you and I Savannah! And I just told you. As a matter of fact, I didn't even *tell* you. Bello just started talking and you saw him," I said, while carefully sliding over to the window where Bello was in an attempt to hide him from Xavier.

"Well, how about *you* start talking *Dylan* and tell me why you haven't told us that you have some extraterrestrial stuff popping off in your room man!" Xavier insisted.

"Extraterrestrial? First, where did you learn that word and second, *that* is a good question," I said with my head hanging low.

Now my secret is out. What do I do? I need Rashidi, my most trusted confidant. I put my thumb in my mouth, time stopped, and thankfully Rashidi appeared.

Chapter 11

Buffoonery

The room turned indigo and all the items stood still. I turned to Xavier and he had a look on his face as if he was trying to eat air. And Savannah was staring at me like I was getting ready to run her over with my BMX bike. I had to chuckle to myself for a minute. I have only seen my parents and my baby sister, Dallas, frozen in time before. I crept into the kitchen to see if my parents were frozen too. They were.

I told Rashidi to turn his head. And as soon as he did, I turned around, bent my knees like my Uncle Lee taught me in baseball, pulled down my pants and mooned the crap out of Savannah and Xavier. That's right, they saw my bare booty! I swung it left and right and up and down. – That's what they get for coming over uninvited and unannounced. Now, I felt vindicated and could get back to business – consulting with Rashidi.

Rashidi looked tired.

"What's the matter Pitter-Patter?" he said with a sassy little voice.

"I'm at a lost for words," I moped.

"A loss for words??? Judging by what you just did, you have also lost your mind? You better be glad they're frozen."

Leaning against my closet Rashidi yawned, "Now, tell me. Why are you *this* upset when you have Miss Savannah in your room along with your best friend? It seems like a win-win Butter-Pin."

"The secret is out the bag, what do I do, what do I do?" I exclaimed in a frustrated tone.

Rashidi guffawed, "What secret? Did you *really* think you would be able to hide the fact that you have a talking lizard AND a talking cat that have lived for millions of years? And most important, that you can travel through time, past and let's not forget future, to participate in Black historic events? And what about that fabulous counselor of yours? Why, oh why, you would want to keep *me* as a secret I do not know Sugar-Dumpling."

Now Rashidi was laughing so hard he no longer looked exhausted. He was actually in tears he was laughing so hard. I mean, doubled over, holding his stomach and was cackling AT me and not WITH me. WOW!

Rashidi caught his breath and said, "Well, look at it this way, you can have company when you travel now. Three heads are better than one any day. Besides, your little adventures have become *boring-boring- boring.* You just blend in and observe. You *never* talk to people. You never make any friends. I mean, how many countries can we visit? How many lakes can we explore? And frankly, I am tired of being awakened for buffoonery."

His mood changed again, and now he seemed irked.

"Buffoonery? What the heck is buffoonery?" I said giggling.

"It's this conversation – bye!" And just like that, he disappeared, and everything was back in motion.

Chapter 12

Pap: 1878*ish*

"Take that nasty thing out of your mouth!" Savannah said with the corner of her lip nearly touching her nose.

"Let's change the subject. Savannah, if you told Xavier everything, then I don't need to tell either one of you anything else. When I go on another adventure I will take you all with me IF you can stay up," I said gazing at them out of the corner of my eyes.

In a French accent Xavier said, "Adventure? Define ad-veeen-ture,"

"I once stayed up until 11:30 when Berny was watching me," confessed Savannah.

"I'm talking about well past that, Savvy."

"Don't call me *Savvy*," Savannah snapped.

It appeared that the name I call her in my head (and what I have her programmed in my cell phone) was not appreciated in real life. I had obviously struck a nerve. But I just let it go – I hope she will too. I would hate to see her leave (with my secret) over something this silly! Not to mention I probably wouldn't have the courage to ask her to come back.

Time passed and the three of us planned our next journey. I explained that I had to return to Nashville to meet up with my friend Pap.

Well, his full name is Benjamin Singleton, but everyone called him Pap. I caught them up to speed about why I needed to return, and how Pap was similar to Harriet Tubman. Except, what *he* was doing was not a secret and it was just for the people moving from the South to Kansas.

I explained that I traveled to eras like 1878 because I only had a little money - to travel from Tennessee to Kansas was only $5.00!

"Five dollars??? To travel over 500 miles? Man, that's dirt-cheap. Yeah, I want to go there – I have like $41 in my sock drawer. I'd be rich!" Xavier said with a little too much enthusiasm if you asked me.

"You can't be out there like a rapper balling out of control Xavier! People would look at you like you were crazy. Right Dylan? We have to blend in. I have some old clothes I can wear tomorrow," she said smiling and playing with her hair beads.

"Here's the thing...I normally stay with old family that my cat locates for me when I travel."

"YOUR WHAT???" – Xavier and Savannah said in unison.

"My cat – never mind that. Look, we're not staying at a high-end hotel. And we may even have to stay at an old converted boarding house for fugitive slaves at some point."

"Hold up – I'm not doing that," Xavier said, acting like he was cutting off his neck with the tips of his fingers.

"Why not?" I asked.

"Because I don't want to is *why not*," he said; this time shoving his hands in his pockets.

"Look Xavier! This is *his* thing – either we go or we don't. I say we go and see what it's all about and then refuse the next adventure if we don't like it. But I must say, I'm not looking forward to pretending to be a slave myself Dylan," Savannah admitted.

"Oh, wait. Slavery was over by this time. This was AFTER the Civil War and after the Reconstruction. We are just staying there until we can get to Cyprus," I assured them both.

"Whew...I was about to say boooooyyyyy," Xavier said jumping up and down.

"What's in Cyprus and is it still around or are we on a mission to try and save it?" Savannah stood up in a superhero stance.

"I'm trying to get in good with Pap..."

"PAP???" – Xavier and Savannah said in unison again.

"Just call that man Mr. Singleton dude," Xavier pleaded.

"Alright. Well, Mr. Singleton owns a place called the Edgefield Real Estate and Homestead Association and I need in on that operation. But, I'm still only nine years old no matter which era I go to," I proclaimed.

"So what! Just go up to him and tell him that you want in on the operation. But, what would a nine-year-old do at a real estate company? Answer phones? Did they have phones back then?"

"Yeah. They've been out for about a year and a half in 1878," I replied.

"Great – We'll both go with you and tell him that you want to work for him, and then we're off to Cyprus. That's the plan – boom. Hands in and let's go," Savannah rushed.

"Wait. No. Stop." I grunted.

"It's not that simple. There are over 30,000 people waiting to go from Nashville to Kansas. I think people looking for a place to call home is more important that me wanting to build a safe house for myself on an island," I confessed.

They never questioned why I needed a safe house and that was fine by me. I didn't want to tell them about Rashidi just yet. Heck, Rashidi is the reason I need to build this safe house. He's so moody – I have a feeling he is going to leave me stranded one day in the past. I desperately need to have a place to go and live for the rest of my life without my parents if he ever does.

The plans were made and the date was set. I told them that I would tell them when it was time to go and that they just need to *stay* ready.

As they were strutting out the door, it hit me. This was the last collaboration project we would have to do for the year. This project would literally be the most defining moment of my life thus far. I mean, I will actually get to see how I work under pressure *and* with a girl.

This was going to be sweeeeet! But until then all I could see in my head was Skyzone in the distance - here we come!

Chapter 13

Understand Without Understanding

The farm *presentation* portion went well. I knew we would get an 'A'. And, I knew that Xavier would take the show during his presentation. He covered all the bases and I learned a lot, as did the rest of the class. We always do when it comes to Xavier. He regularly goes above and beyond on *ad hoc* projects assigned by Ms. Anderson. He just plays so much that I, nor anyone else, ever takes him seriously. I think I am the only one that goes home to fact check what he says during presentations. And believe it or not, he is normally *1,000%* correct.

Now, on to the end of year parent teacher conferences. My mom called my cell phone to say she was going to be a little late, as usual. My dad is always on time. But oddly, neither one of them had shown up yet. I waited outside of Ms. Anderson's room just as they told me to do this morning. I was hoping to hear what Xavier's punishment was going to be for acting so silly during his presentation, that way we could laugh about it. The funny thing is, no matter how much Xavier tries to be popular he doesn't realize that he can be smart *too*. And because he doesn't quite know this yet, Ms. Anderson always has something snarky to say about him. I know he *can't wait* until this year is over.

Suddenly, Xavier's mother came bolting out of the classroom saying, "Lady, you have got to be crazy. My son is only half of the things you're telling me. My baby may *very well* be a class clown. But you left out that he is resourceful, has a wonderful personality, and can read any of these kids under the table. But what he is not, is *un*teachable. You ma'am, need to check yourself."

And just like that they made a left out the door and they never even saw me.

I figured this would be a bad time to ask Xavier to come over and play. So, I quickly jerked my head down and acted like I was reading my book, trying my best not to look up.

"Dylan, are you alone or are your parents parking the car?" she said with the most loving voice.

I can't believe she was so calm after being talked to, or rather, screamed at like that by Xavier's mom.

"My parents aren't here yet. I was just waiting..."

But before I could finish, I saw her rapidly running her fingers down her ponytail and tugging at her skirt.

"Well, hello Mr. Covington. You are always so punctual. And what do I have the pleasure of you coming to see me in uniform?" squealed Ms. Anderson.

What the heck was going on? Why is she talking like my aunts from Atlanta? And what the – why does she keep twitching like she needs to go to pee?

Ewwww, I hope she doesn't like Mr. Covington. That would suck worse than an anteater getting bit by a fire ant *under* his snout if she ended up being Savannah's new mother.

"Hello *Mrs.* Anderson," Mr. Covington said with a smile.

"It's Miss and Anderson is my maiden name," she said blushing and leaning on one leg.

This has got to be the most ridiculous thing I have ever seen in my life. And by the look on Savannah's face, (in addition to the way she is rolling her eyes), she feels the same way.

"Ummm, Dylan. Since your mother is late as usual, would you mind if the lovely Miss Savannah and the handsome, I mean, Sergeant Covington went before you and your notoriously late family?" she said kneeling down rubbing her hands together the way flies do after they throw up on their food.

"Ahhh, sure," I said.

I was so confused. How did this woman go from, nicey-nice-nice to needing to use the bathroom but refusing to go, all the way to looking like a creeper?

"Savannah, why don't you stay out here and keep Dylan company?" she said swiftly pushing the door closed nearly slamming it into Savannah's face.

I didn't think we had a choice is what I wanted to say to her. But my parents wouldn't like that.

I noticed that Savannah was angry. Well, I am not sure if it was anger, or fatigue, or hunger. I didn't know which emotion it was but something was bothering her.

"Look, I'm not still upset about you telling Xavier, okay?" I affirmed.

She looked up at me and asked, "What are you talking about?"

The white of her eyes were red and super shiny. I could see remnants of dried tears on her cheeks and what looked like the stuff that wet Kleenex leaves on her face. But I wasn't sure.

"Have you been practicing staying up late so we can roll out tonight?" I said trying to make her laugh. And just

70

like that, a sea grew in her eyes and tears started falling like raindrops. She stood on her tippy toes, and rested her right ear on her shoulder, reached out, and actually hugged me.

My hands stayed at my side for about two seconds. Just then, my heart plummeted and all I could do was lift my arms and her hug her back. I have never held another girl before other than my little sister Dallas. And I had only hugged my Granny, Grandma, Great-Grandmas, aunts and girl cousins for longer than 30 seconds.

But this was different – and it was okay. I felt a little snot on my shirt but I didn't care. Hey, if she felt comfortable enough to cry on my shoulder, *and* snot up my shirt, then that means I now have a new best friend – and she's a girl. I just listened to her sob and tried to hold back tears of my own. But as the wind blew into the breezeway, I knew it wouldn't be long before I too started to weep with Savannah.

Seconds later, just as I suspected, the north wind whisked through the concrete hollow hallway walls and the sea that built up in my eyes gradually became a river running down my cheeks. We cried together, but I didn't know what *we* were crying about. And I didn't care. I just wanted my friend to understand that I felt her pain too.

Even if I couldn't make it better. I guess when you care about a friend, you can understand without understanding.

And that is exactly what I was doing.

Chapter 14

55,000 things...

"Well, we hate to see you all go Sergeant Covington," Ms. Anderson said shaking her head and holding on to Sergeant Covington's hand way too long.

"Why don't you come over next Thursday night for dinner *Miss* Anderson? There will be moving boxes all over the place but I am sure Savannah would love to spend some time with you outside of school before we go. She always speaks so highly of you," Mr. Covington said gesturing for Savannah to come over to him.

She sauntered toward her father and turned around to look at me. The look on her face said *I don't want to leave you.* I just returned her look of despair with a crooked smile. I felt like we were having an hour-long conversation with just our eyes.

"Why, that sounds delightful. I would be honored," Ms. Anderson answered like a Southern belle.

"Great, we'll see you then," Mr. Covington said, wrapping his arm around Savannah's neck simultaneously as she wrapped hers around his waist while wiping her face on his clean, pressed blue shirt.

I had to find out why she was crying.

I had never called her house before. And this was the last day of the school year. What could I possibly call her and say?

As I was deep in my thoughts, I heard, "Well, I parked it where I normally park it Fred, how was I supposed to know?"

Finally, it was *my* parents. I looked at them, trying to decipher what the fuss was all about. But the way my mother sounded, I had better not. I just sprang up, grabbed my backpack and started walking toward them.

"Boy! Turn around and walk to your class. We're already an hour late!" my mother said with her purse swinging up and down like she was swatting a fly.

"As usual," my father said under his breath.

We both snickered.

"Oh, so you all think this is funny? You two think I do this on purpose? I have 55,000 things to do on a..." My mother was talking so fast.

"Well, hello Starkes family," Ms. Anderson interrupted in the most upbeat voice.

This woman is starting to scare me – now she sounds like she is from New Jersey. She goes from hot to cold in zero point five seconds. It's just plain creepy I tell you!

"Hello Ms. Anderson. I'm sorry I'm – ummm - I mean *we're* late. I had car trouble," my mother said pursing her lips and holding her head towards the sky.

"Yes, if getting your car towed for the third time this year is 'car trouble' then yes – sorry we are late," my dad had the biggest smile on his face while he was looking at my mom and apologizing to Ms. Anderson for their tardiness.

"No worries, no worries at all. I am happy you finally made it. It was getting so cold out there I started to see Dylan's eyes water from the draft in that breezeway," Ms. Anderson remarked caressing my face with the back of her hand.

Really lady? Is what I wanted to say.

"Well now. Come in and let's get started. Here are Dylan's MAPs test results and let me just say he is off the charts. Have you ever thought about putting him in a sport or something to balance out his intellectual activities?" she said primly with her hands pressed together and her head tilted to the side, looking *ever* so concerned.

"Yes. We have looked into soccer for him and basketball, which is my personal favorite. We're also sending him to some overnight camps this summer for him to gain a better foundation of the sports," my dad explained.

"We are?" I glanced over to him pass my mom.

He winked at me and I knew he was covering for me. YES, is all I could think. This summer is going to be s-w-ee-t. I'll be able to travel without being so weary the next day that I could barely keep still!

"I say that because I have recommended a lot of review work for some of my other students for over the summer. BUT, I think Dylan would do good by laying *off* the studies for a while so he can be on the same level with his peers next year. Studies have shown that when you push a child as hard as you push Dylan, they burn out by high school."

Ms. Anderson rambled on and on, flipping through brochure after brochure. I could see my mother's foot swaying back and forth, back and forth. Up and down, up and down. This was NOT good.

That little wrinkle came above my mother's nose, she started waving the palms of her hands in the air and asserted, "Well, Ms. Anderson. We don't *'push'* Dylan at all. He enjoys reading and all things academic. As a matter of fact, it is not school*work* for him. Learning is fun and that is the kind of attitude we try to foster towards *education* at the Starkes residence."

My mother ended her monologue with a confused look on her face. Like she didn't understand what she was saying, but I know my mom did – especially if *I* did.

"Well, Dylan tells me that you two wake up and go over studies in the morning. That sounds a little Tiger-momish don't you think?" Ms. Anderson said shaking her head up and down as if she was trying to get my mother to do the same thing.

"Ms. Anderson," my father said while clearing his throat and interjected, "The early morning wake ups have been going on for years. You see, Dylan is an early riser. So my wife and I decided to capitalize on the quiet time with us not having much of it for Dylan with the arrival of the baby about two years ago. It allows him to do something that he enjoys without being interrupted by his baby sister. Be it reading, math, you know, whatever piques his interest."

My father was fidgeting with his hat and looking Ms. Anderson square in the eye. Then it happened. Instead of her eyelids blinking up and down, like humans, her eyelids never moved and her pupils moved from right to left as if she had reptilian brilles on them. Maybe I was seeing things. But then it happened again. And this time I was sure I saw a nictitating membrane. I looked over at my father and I think he saw it too.

Chapter 15

Hot Breath & Cone Snails

"Ms. Anderson, we would never force our child to do something he does not want to do," my mother assured her.

"I know you wouldn't Mrs. Starkes. Nor am I implying that you would. What I am saying is that, Dylan has already skipped a grade, and the district is not going to allow him to skip another. So, perhaps if you slow his learning down a bit at home and allow us to keep him on track with the rest of the kids in his grade he won't be so bored that he falls asleep in class. And more importantly, he won't burn out as the studies have shown."

"That's not going to happen" my mother said with a smile on her face.

"What part?" Ms. Anderson asked.

"All of it. Any of it. Some of it. And none of it," my mother explained.

"I don't understand Mrs. Starkes. This is a good problem to have," Ms. Anderson responded, looking baffled.

"It may be good for you, because you will always have a student. And, this school will always have someone to boost its test scores. But what does *that* do to Dylan?" she said leaning back in her chair and gripping her handbag. I thought we were getting ready to go and then my mother looked at me and said, "As a matter of fact, Dylan, go wait outside," and she pointed towards the door.

I looked at my dad as if to say *what do I do*? He nodded towards the exit, and so I went.

I stayed out in that breezeway for what felt like an hour. I played with a snail I found buried in the dirt hoping it wasn't a cone snail. You know, the ones that bite you and suck you in and then you're gone from the planet?

Then I remembered cone snail only live in water. I got *so* bored that I cleaned off the emergency glass of the fire extinguisher six times with my hot breath and fingers. I was just so worried – it was getting dark and no one had come to check on me.

Then I remembered - BELLO.

I knocked on the door and asked if I could come in to see if I left something. This way, I could go in and put Bello under my dad's seat. I think I was too late because I heard the word "homeschool" and stopped in my tracks.

"You are going to do what?" I bellowed.

My parent's heads jolted in my direction and they looked at me like I was an alien from another planet.

"Why are you in here Dylan? I told you to wait outside sweetheart," my mother said.

"I was, and then I realized I left something so..." my mother cut me off.

"We are having an adult conversation and we would appreciate if you would wait outside for us to finish it."

"But this conversation is about me. It is regarding me. And it sounds like it will ultimately affect ME. Why can't I be in here?" I said with a shaky voice.

"Good question Dylan, have a seat," Ms. Anderson offered.

"Honey, how would you feel about leaving *all* of your friends and *all* of your teachers and the *nice* lunch lady who always gives you seconds and our library with *all* the books you can read that opens at 7:00 a.m. and not 11:00 a.m. and has no late fees for your mom to pay to be homeschooled?" Ms. Anderson asked that run-on sentence waaaaaay too close to my face AND without taking any pauses.

And ewww, her breath smelled like ginger and copper.

"What does that mean?" I said moving back a little.

"It means you should go outside and let us finish up this conversation with your teacher, son," my dad said.

My dad looked at me as if he was going to run me out of the classroom. And so again I went. I sat outside, never even getting the chance to plant Bello to be my spy. I felt helpless. What is homeschooling? What do they do? How am I going to have school at home? Is a teacher going to come and teach me? Is Ms. Anderson right?

Will I leave *all* my friends and this wonderful library to sit at the house being pestered by Dallas and having to go to the grocery store with my mom and her friend, Ms. Angie, every Wednesday?

81

I can't believe it but now *I* want to cry. I want to cry and I want to run away. What have I done *so bad* that I can't go to school anymore?

Chapter 16

Ignored, Cagey, and Unwanted

First Day of Summer

I normally wake up on the first day of summer to the kitchen being packed with all my favorites. My mom and I make a huge breakfast while jamming out to the peanut butter jelly song. We dance all over the kitchen while the song loops over and over again until we're done and ready to eat. But this morning was different.

My dad was in the kitchen with the paper and NOT at work. And my sister was actually siting in front of the TV. It was the first day of summer dang-it. I *just know* there are some kids who need to be taken to summer camp. And I'm almost positive the phones are ringing off the hook. What the heck was my dad doing home? Something was seriously wrong.

This was ruining my entire first day of summer ritual. I wondered if my mom and dad had a disagreement last night, or worse, if my dad lost his job. No way...we own the company that transports children in limos and buses.

"Good morning?" I said in a reluctant voice.

My dad grunted something that sounded like good morning and my mother never looked up from her computer. Even Dallas didn't say anything to me. I walked over to my mother and gave her a side hug just to spy and see what she was working on *or* reading.

She quickly closed the computer but I saw something that looked like a Facebook page with a bunch of likes. There was a black chalkboard and I couldn't make it all out but it looked like it said, *"African American Homeschool Moms."*

"Where is my phone?" my mother asked.

Without looking up from his paper my dad replied, "On the charger."

I had to find out what she was looking at and why she was being so cagey about it. She scooted back from the table, buried her head into the palms of her hands and ran her index fingers over her eyebrows. I knew that this was *not* good. My mother is usually VERY happy in the morning.

"Did you sleep well?" I asked, trying to read her face for any signs of *Dylan you 'gon' get it* written anywhere on it.

I couldn't make out anything.

"Hello, may I speak to the principal please?" She paused. "Yes, this is Mrs. Starkes, I am Dylan Starkes' mother."

My heart started palpitating. I thought school was closed!!!! I headed to the family room to plop down next to my sister but she too didn't want me to see what she was doing. I want answers.

"No, Die-yeen! This is my show," she said pushing me away.

I headed towards my father. But I knew that if I got him to start talking, I wouldn't be able to hear what my mother was saying. So, I did what any smart kid would do, I pretended to go to the bathroom and I took Bello in there with me to devise a scheme.

Chapter 17

Knock, Knock

The plan was set in motion. Bello was going to see what was going on. *My right hand man.* He slithered into the dining room and listened. I didn't hear my mom complaining about him so, one - I knew he had made it in without her noticing, and two - the plan was a go. There was a lot of silence. So much, that my dad asked was I all right in there. I said yes and anxiously waited for Bello to return. And when he did, I didn't know whether to be devastated or elated.

"Well, your mom and dad are serious about homeschooling you and you are officially checked out of Grand Elementary School," Bello announced reluctantly.

"What does that mean? So, I'm just going to be out gallivanting in the streets of Los Angeles while everyone else is learning? Or will I get to go to Magic Mountain while everyone else is learning? I'm confused," I said straddling the toilet seat with my head down.

"Look, you didn't do anything wrong and this is not a punishment – as a matter of fact, I think it's pretty cool!

There are a million kids who *wish* they could be sitting on the toilet as long as you were to get this kind of news," Bello said climbing onto my shoulder.

"What?" I said trying to cheer up.

"Not sitting on the toilet constipated or anything like that – you know what I mean!" he chuckled.

"Dylan, just go to your mom, flash those perfect chops and give her that *'I'm your little man'* stance that Jack does from the show *Blackish* and say, 'Mommy – what's going on?' Now, of course she may look at you like you're crazy, especially if she has the phone to her ear OR in her hands, but it won't hurt anything," Bello urged in the most sincere voice I had ever heard him use.

And he was right, all I had to do was go in there and talk to her. She was a reasonable woman. The only time I have ever seen her come out of *mommy character* is when some lady asked to touch her hair in Target. All I needed were answers to my questions and she's a *great* explainer.

I walked past the living room, into the kitchen and poured my mom some more coffee.

"Hey mom, I poured you a fresh cup of coffee," I announced with a smile.

She intensely scanned my face with her eyes, touched my nose, and kissed my forehand and sighed, "Thank you baby."

"No problem. *SO* what's going on? Why were you calling the school on summer break?" I asked.

"Well I just wanted to talk to the..."

There was a knock at the door. I bet it was Xavier coming to eat "first day of summer" breakfast with me. I walked over to answer it. And although I never heard or saw my dad get up from the table, I immediately felt his hands resting on my shoulders moving me to the side.

"I got this little man."

My dad opened the door and my stomach fell all the way down to my knees, my armpits started to sweat, and all I saw was Ms. Anderson and Principal Humphries smiling from ear to ear. I was stuck. I felt like my feet were in tar. I could not move. Ms. Anderson looked at me and I saw her tongue – IT HAD A SPLIT IN IT!

"Hello Mr. Starkes. I know that we did not call, but we wanted to talk to you and your wife about Dylan," she said looking into the living room.

"I just want to let you know that no matter what you do, where you go, and what you say, Dylan *will* be back to Grand Elementary next year. We will do everything in our power to make sure of it. We will see to it that he is kept in an environment where he is challenged and cared for emotionally. We just really want you to know that we are on *your* side," she said clutching her brief bag.

"Oh, really, then what would possess you to come to my house unannounced? If you cared about my son's emotional state, you would have called first. He is terrified," my mother said picking up my sister from the floor and pulling me closer to her.

"My son does not do well with surprises, or people who come over unannounced He likes structure and predictability," my mother said.

With a catch in my voice I said, "I'm not afraid Mom."

"Good! Dylan, do you mind if I see your awesome room while Principal Humphries speaks with your parents," Ms. Anderson asked.

I don't know why I did it. But I said, "Sure, it's this way," and led her towards my room.

Chapter 18

Feat

Ms. Anderson pushed the door closed softly. And then she pounced toward me. I tried to run for the door, but she managed to grab me by the arm.

"Why are you grabbing my arm? Let go of me!" I screamed.

"You *are* going to school! All day! Everyday! AND you WILL enjoy it," Ms. Anderson sneered.

I wondered why my parents couldn't hear me. This woman was crazy. Then, unexpectedly, Ms. Anderson's body began to change. First, her feet got small. Then, her eyes turned reptilian. I could now see her nictitating membrane up close and in full view. I couldn't believe all this was happening to her and she still managed to have my dang arm!

She started breathing extra heavy, and fast, and then her hair changed from a neat ponytail with bangs to this long silky stuff that looked like yarn. Her teeth transformed from off white to a greyish hue and her gums were green???

Luckily all her clothes stayed on.

I thought her heart was going to rip through her chest and just dangle out of her body. But it wasn't an organ at all. It was a badge that read

"THE SCHOOL RETENTION LEAGUE".

What the??? I tried to run to my closet. But she was too quick. Her long tail hit the door. There was no way I was going to get in there. I yelled the word *ENYEMAKA*, the Igbo word for help, and both Sanura and Bello sprang into action.

Sanura lunged toward her and sliced her across the eye with one paw and dug her claws into Ms. Anderson's neck with the other. I thought that would have slowed her down but it just made her more furious. *Both* her eyes started bleeding and she let out a maniacal laugh as she released my arm and threw me against my door. Slowly she slithered up my wall, onto the ceiling and dangled her head down in front of my face.

She slurred her words and spoke like a snake, "Sooooooo, you are one of the sssssspecial onesssss. You have help? Well, they won't be able to help you from ussssss!"

I looked around for Bello and couldn't spot him anywhere. I turned my back and tried to open the door but she thrust her tongue out of her mouth and pulled me back by my neck and lifted me off the ground. I tried to break free but she was shaking me too hard. I cried out for my parents. They didn't answer. Every time I tried to stick my thumb in my mouth she jerked me harder.

The room started to fade out. I couldn't take it anymore. Sanura's bites and scrapes were doing nothing to her.

I let out a final plea of help, "Bello – help me!"

"Bite her – bite her as hard as you can when I tell you," he commanded.

I was gasping for air and said, "I can't bite her – her tongue is around my neck."

I didn't know where Bello was. Everything was getting darker. I couldn't hold on any longer. Just then, Sanura pounced onto the top of Ms. Anderson's tail, buried her claws deep inside her flesh and slid down. Blood was everywhere! First it was blue, then it turned green and then it dissipated into some sort of slimy clear water all over my room.

I could hear Bello in the distance, "Hold your hand out. And when Sanura says '*now*' slice her tongue but watch your neck."

This was the scariest thing I ever had to do in my life. Suddenly I felt something in my hand. It was a knife. Bellow transformed into a knife to save my life.

"Now!" Sanura yelled. My body was weak, but I gripped the knife as hard as I could, and sliced her nasty, smelly, rough, tongue like I was a samurai then I dropped the knife – I was exhausted. She fell with it, right on her head and me on my butt.

She moaned and I felt her grip ease from my trachea. Bello turned back into a lizard but I couldn't see where he went.

"Now, pull her tongue from your neck!" Bello urged.

He sounded closer this time.

"Now!" Bello screamed.

This time I moved my head to the side, turned my head and bit the little part of her tongue that I could and I didn't let go. I pulled her liver-smelling tongue from around my neck and I was free. Ms. Anderson lifted her head toward the heavens, opened her snout, and let out a mammoth roar.

As she opened her mouth wider and wider, Bello let go of what looked like a week's worth of urates into her mouth from the ceiling. It was the *grossest* thing I had ever seen in my life. I literally threw up in my mouth and swallowed it back down.

Ms. Anderson looked like she was actually swallowing Bello's poop, and was enjoying it – Oooooo this woman was na-ahs-tee! I didn't have time to see just how nasty she was, because I didn't have time for her to retaliate. I ran and slid under my bed like it was first base and jammed my thumb inside my mouth.

Thankfully, time stopped, and Rashidi appeared.

Chapter 19

It Came, You Saw, Now Conquer

Dazed and confused I panted, "I need your help! Ms. Anderson changed into a monster of some sort."

"She is no monster – she is a member of one of the most secretive groups in history, the School Retention League."

"Who are they?"

"The School Retention League I told you – stay with me Dylan," he said obviously trying to be funny.

Now was not the time for his bravado.

"I heard you the first time. What do they do?"

"They will stop at nothing to get bright children such as yourself to stay in traditional school," he said, filing his nails.

"Well, I don't care where she is from, I need her out of my house – the woman is cray-cray!"

"*You* are the one who's cray-cray! Do you understand how lucky you are to be hunted by her kind? You are going to be homeschooled! This is something to be proud about and one of the biggest decisions and sacrifices your family has ever made outside of having YOU and that little booger-eating sister of yours! Annnnnnd being homeschooled is a gift better than ANYTHING you have ever gotten for all of your birthdays put together. Stop being a "scaredy-cat" and give the woman your arm Dylan!" he brayed.

I could feel a knot in my throat – I *was* scared. But I was nobody's "scaredy-cat."

"Besides, there's really no way around this. She *is* going to plant the electronic chip somewhere inside you and she will then know your every move," he said leisurely flying about the room pretending to smell and taste the clear *blood*.

"I'm talking latitude and longitude. Her people practically held the Department of Defense's hand when they invented the navigation system. Don't feel bad though. They do it to all children who talk about homeschooling. There are over a hundred *very informative* articles about it on RaisingBoysHomeschool.com regarding how to prevent this very thing from happening. But it appears to be too late for you," Rashidi said nonchalantly.

"Why are you so calm about this Rashidi? You act like she is your BFF. Almost like you know her personally. Or worse, like you don't care about me," I said with tears in my eyes.

"I *do* care about you. The question is, do YOU care about you?"

"Of course I care about me. I'm trying to get away from her aren't I?"

"Dylan, you need to answer the question of who you are in relation to the *SRL*"

"What is the *SRL*?"

"The School Retention League – stay with me Dylan. You also need to find out who *they* are and what *they* want. In addition to that, you need to find out who *you* are and want *you* want. And lastly, you need to find out if the SRL *NEEDS* you or if they *WANT* you. Annnnnndddd judging by how scary *you* are, you are going to need a little help," he said, looking me up and down with a look of disgust on his face.

Everything he just said was so confusing. I didn't understand nearly half of it - he said it so fast.

I eased down onto the floor with my back against the closet door and held my head low. So low that my chin touched my chest. I had no idea what to do. Do I restart time and let her place a chip in me? Or, do I run away?

Either way, Rashidi was right...I needed help. I started making my way to my closet but Ms. Anderson was frozen right in front of it. So instead, I climbed out the window, into the backyard and went through the wooden door with foliage starting to grow ever so perfectly at the top making my way to Xavier, Savannah and any other friend I could find to help me fight off the School Retention League.

Just as I pushed back this wooden door with exactly seven beams of wood on each side and two horizontal bars, the brightest light shined through. The light looked familiar. It was the same light I saw while being taken up by the tree in South Africa. I knew then I was on the right path! I must find out who the SRL is, how to fight them, and I would need a team.

I began my quest to form The Time Team! T3.

I now understand why the voice in South Africa said,

"When something is out to get you, you have to learn everything you can about it in order to rise above it and conquer it."

And in this case, I needed to learn more about, find, and conquer *the truth*. I needed to find the origin of the SRL and I needed to stop *it* before *it* stopped me. Conquering this mystery will be a feat for us, but hey, we're kids, we have nothing but time!

The End?

Visit www.TheTimeTeamBooks.com for more!

For Further Reading By Subject

Social Studies

US HISTORY: RECONSTRUCTION PERIOD

Title: Exodusters: Black Migration to Kansas After Reconstruction
Author: Painter, Nell Irvin
ISBN: 0394402537

WORLD HISTORY/GOVERNMENT: PASS LAWS

Title: Kaffir Boy: An Autobiography – The True Story of a Black Youth's Coming of Age in Apartheid South Africa
Author: Mathabane, Mark
ISBN: 978-0684848280

GEOGRAPHY: CYPRUS

Title: DK Eyewitness Travel Guide: Cyprus
Author: N/A
ISBN: 978-1465411921

Science

PHYSICS: LIGHT AND TEMPURATURE

Title: Basic Physics: A Self-Teaching Guide
Author: Kahn, Karl
ISBN: 978-047113447

Videos

Search for: Book One - The Beginning by The Time Team Book Series

Titles are shown exactly how it is listed on YouTube and are not typos.

Glossary

Chapter 1

Annoy (verb): to cause (someone) to feel slightly angry

Apparent (adjective): easy to see or understand

Argue (verb): to give reason for or against: to say or write things in order to change someone's opinion about what is true, what should be done, etc.

Contest (verb): to make (something) the subject of an argument or a legal case: to say that you do not agree with or accept (something)

Grip (verb/noun/adjective): to grab or hold something tightly

Immediate (adjective): happening or done without delay

Sauerkraut (noun): a German food made of vegetable (called a cabbage) that is cut into small pieces and soaked in a salty and sour liquid

Seep (verb): to flow or pass slowly through small openings in something.

Chapter 2

Agriculture (noun): the science or occupation of farming

Articulate (verb): able to express ideas clearly and effectively in speech or writing

Comfortable: (adjective): not causing any physically unpleasant feelings : producing physical comfort

Confidence (noun): a feeling or belief that you can do something well or succeed at something

Deceive (verb): to make (someone) believe something that is not true

Glare (noun): to shine with a harsh, bright light

Gnarl (noun): bumpy or twisted

Grumble (verb): to complain quietly about something : to talk in an unhappy way

Hallucinate (verb): to see or sense something or someone that is not really there : to have hallucinations

Howl (verb): to make a long, loud cry that sounds sad

Index-finger (noun): the finger next to the thumb

Introvert (noun): a shy person : a quiet person who does not find it easy to talk to other people

Mesmerize (verb): to hold the attention of (someone) entirely : to interest or amaze (someone) so much that nothing else is seen or noticed — usually used as *(be) mesmerized*

Mutter *(verb):* to speak quietly so that it is difficult for other people to hear what you say

Physics (noun): a science that deals with matter and energy and the way they act on each other in heat, light, electricity, and sound

Prissy (adjective): having or showing the annoying attitude of people who care too much about dressing and behaving properly and who are easily upset by other people's behavior, language, etc.

Radiant (adjective): having or showing an attractive quality of happiness, love, health, etc.

Reflect (verb): to move in one direction, hit a surface, and then quickly move in a different and usually opposite direction

Regal (adjective): of, relating to, or suitable for a king or queen

Ridiculous (adjective): extremely silly or unreasonable

Sequin (noun): a small piece of shiny metal or plastic that is sewn onto clothes as a decoration

Slither (verb): to move by sliding your entire body back and forth

Smug (adjective): disapproving : having or showing the annoying quality of people who feel very pleased or satisfied with their abilities, achievements, etc.

Squeal (verb): to make or cause (something) to make a long, high-pitched cry or noise

Suggest (verb): to mention (something) as a possible thing to be done, used, thought about, etc.

Syllable (noun): any one of the parts into which a word is naturally divided when it is pronounced

Ultraviolet (adjective): used to describe rays of light that cannot be seen and that are slightly shorter than the rays of violet light

Urate: Urine and stool production: Generally speaking, reptile waste has three components: a clear, liquid urine, a chalky white urate (both products of the kidney), and a blackish-brown fecal material. In most cases they are evacuated together. When reptiles are housed in relatively unchanging captive conditions, are fed at regular intervals and are kept in an optimal environment, their bowel movements can become highly predictable. Read more at: https://tr.im/Ze7YL

Chapter 3

Animation (noun): a lively or excited quality

Compost (noun): a decayed mixture of plants (such as leaves and grass) that is used to improve the soil in a garden

Daydream (verb): to think pleasant thoughts about your life or future while you are awake

Disappoint (verb): to make (someone) unhappy by not being as good as expected or by not doing something that was hoped for or expected

Gyrate (verb): to move back and forth in a circular motion

Interject (verb): to interrupt what someone else is saying with (a comment, remark, etc.)

Introduce (verb): to make (someone) known to someone else by name

Scold (verb): to speak in an angry or critical way to (someone who has done something wrong)

Stun (verb): to surprise or upset (someone) very much

Chapter 4

Alarm (verb): a feeling of fear caused by a sudden sense of danger

Announce (verb): to make (something) known in a public or formal way : to officially tell people about (something)

Annoy (verb): to cause (someone) to feel slightly angry

Condescend (adjective/verb): to show that you believe you are more intelligent or better than other people

Confidence (noun): a feeling or belief that you can do something well or succeed at something

Dissolve (verb): of something solid : to mix with a liquid and become part of the liquid

Exclaim (verb): to say (something) in an enthusiastic or forceful way

Jolt (verb/noun): to cause (something or someone) to move in a quick and sudden way

**Mumble** (<u>verb</u>/noun): to say (something) quietly in an unclear way that makes it difficult for people to know what you said

Chapter 5

**Accuse** (<u>verb</u>/noun): to blame (someone) or something wrong or illegal : to say that someone is guilty of a fault or crime

**Anthropomorphism** (adjective): described or thought of as being like human beings in appearance, behavior, etc.

**Concern:** (verb/noun/adjective): a feeling of worry usually shared by many people

**Crooked** (<u>adjective</u>/noun): not straight

**Embarrass** (verb): to make (someone) feel confused and foolish in front of other people

**Glare:** (<u>verb</u>/noun): to look directly at someone in an angry way

**Jerk:** (noun/<u>verb</u>): a quick pull or twist

**Reverberation** (noun): a sound that echoes

Situation (noun): all of the facts, conditions, and events that affect someone or something at a particular time and in a particular place

Thump (<u>verb</u>/noun): to hit or beat something or someone and make a loud, deep sound

Chapter 6

Dentures (noun): a set of artificial (fake) teeth — usually plural

Mechanical (adjective): of or relating to machinery

Minor (<u>adjective</u>/noun/verb): not very important or valuable

Realize (verb): to understand or become aware of (something)

Sniffle (<u>verb</u>/noun): to repeatedly take air into your nose in short breaths that are loud enough to be heard because you are sick or have been crying

Chapter 7

Anguish (noun): extreme suffering, grief, or pain

Confess (verb): to admit you did something wrong or illegal

Despicable (adjective): very bad or unpleasant : deserving to be despised

Devastate (verb): to destroy much or most of (something) : to cause great damage or harm to (something)

Embarrass (verb): to make (someone) feel confused and foolish in front of other people

Immediate: (adjective): happening or done without delay

Irrational (adjective): not thinking clearly : not able to use reason or good judgment

Maniacal (adjective): a person who behaves in a very wild way

Minion (noun): someone who is not powerful or important and who obeys the orders of a powerful leader or boss

Offend (verb): to cause (a person or group) to feel hurt, angry, or upset by something said or done

Pace (noun/<u>verb</u>): to walk back and forth across the same space again and again especially because you are nervous

Pout (verb): to push out your lips to show that you are angry or annoyed

Ramble (verb/<u>noun</u>): a long speech or piece of writing that goes from one subject to another without any clear purpose or direction

Transform (verb): to change (something) completely and usually in a good way

Tremble (verb): to shake slightly because you are afraid, nervous, excited, etc.

Windowpane (noun): a piece of glass that covers an opening in a window

Chapter 8

Abyss (noun): a hole so deep or a space so great that it cannot be measured

Ancient (adjective): very old : having lived or existed for a very long time

Appear (verb): to seem to be something : to make someone think that a person or thing has a particular

Apprehensive (adjective): afraid that something bad or unpleasant is going to happen : feeling or showing fear or apprehension about the future

Assistant (noun): a person who helps someone

Bow (verb/noun): to bend forward at the neck or waist as a formal way of greeting someone or showing respect

Confuse (verb): to make (someone) uncertain or unable to understand something

Demented (adjective): not able to think clearly or to understand what is real and what is not real : crazy or insane

Enthusiastically (adjective): feeling or showing strong excitement about something : filled with or marked by enthusiasm

Flop (verb): to fall, lie, or sit down in a sudden, awkward, or relaxed way

Inaugurate (verb): to introduce (someone, such as a newly elected official) into a job or position with a formal ceremony

Inquisitive (adjective): tending to ask questions : having a desire to know or learn more

Negative (adjective/noun): harmful or bad : not wanted

Obvious (adjective): easy to see or notice

Pact (noun): a formal agreement between two countries, people, or groups especially to help each other or to stop fighting

Particular (adjective/noun): used to indicate that one specific person or thing is being referred to and no others

Pluck (verb/noun): to pull (something) quickly to remove it

Pretend (verb/adjective): to act as if something is true when it is not

__Repeal__ (verb): to officially make (a law) no longer valid

__Respect__ (<u>noun</u>/verb/adjective): a feeling of admiring someone or something that is good, valuable, important, etc.

__Reveal__ (verb): to make (something) known

__Supposed__ (adjective): claimed to be true or real — used to say that a particular description is probably not true or real even though many people believe that it is

__Suspicious__ (adjective): causing a feeling that something is wrong or that someone is behaving wrongly : causing suspicion

Chapter 9

Amuse (verb): to make someone laugh or smile : to entertain (someone) in a light and pleasant way

Canvas (noun): a strong, rough cloth that is used to make bags, tents, sails, paint on etc.

Coarse (adjective): made up of large pieces; not fine

Confuse (adjective/verb): unable to understand or think clearly

Corny (adjective): old-fashioned and silly or sentimental

Exactly (adverb): used to stress that something is accurate, complete, or correct

Expect (verb): to think that something will probably or certainly happen

Feast (noun/verb): a special meal with large amounts of food and drink

__Gesture__ (noun/<u>verb</u>): to make a gesture : to move your hands, arms, etc., to express an idea or feeling

__Gleam__ (noun/<u>verb</u>): to shine brightly

__Horror__ (verb/<u>adjective</u>/noun): intended to cause feelings of fear or horror

__Literally__ (adverb): in a literal way: such as : in a way that uses the ordinary and usual meaning of a word

__Motivate__ (verb) : to give (someone) a reason for doing something

__Nod__ (<u>verb</u>/noun): to move your head up and down as a way of answering "yes" or of showing agreement, understanding, or approval

__Opportunity__ (noun): chance; an amount of time or a situation in which something can be done

__Plead__ (verb): to ask for something in a serious and emotional way

__Pressure__ (<u>noun</u>/verb): the weight or force that is produced when something presses or pushes against something else

__Reconstruction__ (noun): The **period** after the Civil War, 1865 - 1877, was called the **Reconstruction period**. Abraham Lincoln started planning for the **reconstruction** of the South during the Civil War as Union soldiers occupied huge areas of the South.

__Retrieve__ (verb): to get and bring (something) back from a place

__Snicker__ (verb): to make a short, quiet laugh in a way that shows disrespect

__Stagger__ (verb/noun/<u>adjective</u>): extremely shocked or surprised

__Stormed__ (noun/verb): to go quickly and in an angry, loud way

__Venture__ (<u>verb</u>/noun): to go somewhere that is unknown, dangerous, etc.

Chapter 10

Appeared (verb): to seem to be something : to make someone think that a person or thing has a particular characteristic

Attempt (verb/noun): to try to do (something) : to try to accomplish or complete something

Cot (noun): a narrow, light bed often made of cloth stretched over a folding frame

Extraterrestrial (adjective): coming from or existing outside the planet Earth

Inhaler (noun): a device used for inhaling a medication

Secrecy (noun): the act of keeping information secret

Chapter 11

__Adventure__ (noun): an exciting or dangerous experience

__Buffoonery__ (noun): silly, foolish behavior that is meant to be funny

__Cackle__ (verb): to laugh noisily

__Counselor__ (noun): a person who provides advice as a job : a person who counsels people

__Consult__ (verb): to go to (someone, such as a doctor or lawyer) for advice : to ask for the professional opinion of (someone)

__Crept__ (verb): to move slowly with the body close to the ground

__Exhausted__ (verb/noun): to use all of someone's mental or physical energy : to tire out or wear out (someone) completely

__Frustrated__ (adjective/verb): very angry, discouraged, or upset because of being unable to do or complete something

Historic (adjective): famous or important in history

Indigo (noun): a deep purplish-blue color

Moped (verb): to behave in a way that shows you are unhappy and depressed

Sassy (adjective): having or showing a rude or lack of respect

Unannounced (adjective): surprising and unexpected : not having been announced or spoken about before

Chapter 12

Accent (noun): a way of pronouncing words that occurs among the people in a particular region or country

Ancestors (noun): a person who was in someone's family in past times : one of the people from whom a person is descended

Appear (verb): to seem to be something : to make someone think that a person or thing has a particular characteristic

Collaboration (verb): to work with another person or group in order to achieve or do something

Confess (verb): to admit that you did something wrong or illegal

Cyprus (noun): a country in Europe: Cyprus, an island in the eastern Mediterranean, has rich, turbulent history stretching back to antiquity. Known for its beaches, it has a rugged interior with wine-growing regions. It's separated into a Greek south and Turkish north, with the capital Nicosia also divided.

__Defining__ (adjective): the month that showed very clearly what kind of thing it is

__Distance__ (__noun__/verb): the amount of space between two places or things

__Fugitive__ (__noun__/adjective): a person who is running away to avoid being captured

__Gaze__ (__verb__/noun): to look at someone or something in a steady way and usually for a long time.

__Moody__ (adjective): often unhappy or unfriendly

__Obvious__ (adjective): easy to see or notice

Chapter 13

__Ad hoc__ (adjective): formed or used for a special purpose

__Concrete__ (<u>noun</u>/adjective/verb): a hard, strong material that is used for building and made by mixing cement, sand, and broken rocks with water

__Conference__ (noun): a formal meeting in which many people gather in order to talk about ideas or problems related to a particular topic

__Gradually__ (adjective): moving or changing in small amounts: happening in a slow way over a long period of time.

__Hollow__ (<u>adjective</u>/noun/verb): having nothing inside : not solid

__Maiden Name__ (noun): a woman's (family) last name before she is married

__Notorious__ (noun): Well-known or famous especially for something bad

__Personality__ (noun): the set of emotional qualities, ways of behaving, etc., that makes a person different from other people.

Plummet (verb): to fall suddenly straight down especially from a very high place.

Presentation (noun): an activity in which someone shows, describes, or explains something to a group of people.

Punctual (adjective): arriving or doing something at the expected or planned time

Punishment (noun): the act of punishing someone or a way of punishing someone

Remnants (noun): the part of something that is left when the other parts are gone

Resourceful (adjective): able to deal well with new or difficult situations and to find solutions to problems

Suspect (very/<u>noun</u>/adjective): a person who is believed to be possibly guilty of committing a crime

Whisk (noun/<u>verb</u>): to move to take someone or something to another place very quickly

Chapter 14

__Brille__ (noun): The **brille** (also called the **ocular scale**, **eye cap** or **spectacle**) is the layer of transparent, immovable disc-shaped skin or scale covering the eyes of some animals for protection, especially in animals without eyelids. The brille has evolved from a fusion of the upper and lower eyelids. Brille means "spectacles" or "<u>glasses</u>" in German, Norwegian and Danish and "shine" in French and Spanish

__Brochure__ (noun): a small, thin book or magazine that usually has many pictures and information about a product, a place, etc.

__Caress__ (noun/<u>verb</u>): a gentle loving touch

__Crooked__ (<u>adjective</u>/noun): not straight

*__Deciphe__*r (verb): to find the meaning of something

__Intellectual__ (<u>adjective</u>/noun): of or relating to the ability to think in a logical way

__Interject__ (verb): to interrupt what someone else is saying with (a comment, remark, etc.)

__Interrupt__ (verb): to ask questions or say things while another person is speaking; to do or say something that causes someone to stop speaking

__Membrane__ (noun): a thin sheet or layer

__Nictitating__ (noun): The **nictitating membrane** (from Latin *nictare*, to blink) is a transparent or translucent third eyelid present in some animals that can be drawn across the eye for protection and to moisten it while maintaining visibility.

__Primly__ (adjective): sometimes disapproving, very formal and proper

__Pupil__ (noun): (2nd definition) – the small, black, round, area at the center of the eye.

__Purse__ (noun): a usually leather or cloth bag used by women for carrying money and personal things; handbag

__Remark__ (noun/verb): to make a statement about something or someone

__Saunter__ (verb): to walk in a slow and relaxed manner

__Simultaneous__ (adjective): happening at the same time

__Snicker__ (verb): to make a short, quiet laugh in a way that shows disrespect

Supposed (adjective): claimed to be true or real — used to say that a particular description is probably not true or real even though many people believe that it is

Wrinkle (<u>noun</u>/verb/adjective): a small line that appears on your skin as you grow older

Chapter 15

Appreciate (verb): to understand the worth of (something or someone) : to admire and value (something or someone)

Assure (verb): toe make (something) certain

Breezeway (noun): a narrow structure with a roof and no walls that connects two buildings (such as a house or a garage)

Conversation (noun): an informal talk involving two people or a small group of people : the act of talking in an informal way

Extinguisher (noun): a metal container filled with chemicals that is used to put out a fire

Ginger (noun/verb): the strongly flavored root of a tropical plants that is used in cooking

Imply (verb): to express (something) in an indirect way : to suggest (something) without saying or showing it plainly

Important (adjective): having serious meaning or worth

Jolt (verb/noun): to cause (something or someone) to move in a quick and sudden way)

Pester (verb): to annoy or bother (someone) in a repeated way

Respond (verb): to say or write something as an answer to a question or request

Spy (noun/verb): (2nd definition) – someone who secretly watches the movement or actions of other people

Chapter 16

Argument (noun) a statement or series of statement for or against something

Bury (verb): (2nd definition [b]) – to hide (something) so that it cannot be seen or is difficult to see

Cagey (adjective): not willing to say everything that you know about something

Grunt (verb): a short low sound from the throat

Ignore (verb): to refuse to show that you hear or see (something or someone)

Palpitate (verb): to beat quickly and strongly and often in a way that is not regular because of excitement, nervousness, etc.

Pretend (verb/adjective): to act as if something is true when it is not

Reluctant (adjective): feeling or showing doubt about doing something : not willing or eager to do something

Ritual (noun/adjective): a formal ceremony or series of acts that is always performed in the same way

Ruin (verb/noun): to damage (something) so badly that it is no longer useful, valuable, enjoyable, etc. : to spoil or destroy (something)

Scoot (verb): to go or leave suddenly and quickly
Transport (verb): to carry (someone or something) from one place to anther)

Chapter 17

___Announce___ (verb): to make (something) known in a public or formal way : to officially tell people about (something)

___Anxious___ (adjective): afraid or nervous especially about what may happen : feeling anxiety

___Complain___ (verb): to say or write that you are unhappy, sick, uncomfortable, etc., or that you do not like something

___Devastate___ (verb): (2nd definition) – to cause someone to feel extreme emotional pain

___Gallivant___ (verb): to go or travel to many different places for pleasure

___Intense___ (adjective): very great in degree : very strong

___Reluctant___ (adjective): feeling or showing doubt about doing something : not willing or eager to do something

___Scan___ (verb/noun): to look at (something) carefully usually in order to find someone or something

Slither (verb): to move by sliding your entire body back and forth

Straddle (verb): to sit or ride with a leg on either side of (something)

Chapter 18

Feat (noun): an act or achievement that shows courage, strength, or skill

Hue (noun): a color or a shade of a color

Igbo (noun): The **Igbo** people, historically spelled "Ibo", are an ethnic group of southeastern Nigeria. They speak **Igbo**, which includes various Igboid languages and dialects. **Igbo** people are one of the largest ethnic groups in Africa.

Pounce (verb): to suddenly jump toward and take hold of something or someone

Retention (noun): the act of keeping someone or something

Transform (verb): to change (something) completely and usually in a good way

Unexpectedly (adjective): no expected

Chapter 19

Beams (noun): (2nd definition) – a long and heavy piece of wood or metal that is used as a support in a building or ship

Conquer (verb): to take control of through the use of force : to defeat through use of force : to gain control of (a problem or difficultly) through great effort

Foliage (noun): the leaves of a plant or of many plants

Horizontal (adjective): positioned from side to side rather than up and down : parallel to the ground

Latitude (noun): distance north or south of the equator measured in degrees up and 90 degrees : an imaginary line that circles the Earth at a particular latitude and that is parallel to the equator

Longitude (noun): distance measured in degrees east or west from an imaginary line (called the prime meridian) that goes from the North Pole to the South Pole and that passes through Greenwish, England : an imaginary line that circles the Earth at a particular longitude

__Nonchalantly__ (adjective): relaxed and calm in a way that shows that you do not care or are worried about anything

__Obviously__ (adjective): easy to see or notice

__Practically__ (adverb): almost or nearly

__Quest__ (noun/verb): a journey made in search of something

__Relation__ (noun): (2nd definition) – the way in which two or more things are connected

__Traditional__ (adjective): (2nd definition) – based on old-fashioned ideas : not new, different, or modern